My First Book About the
Internet

Written by Sharon Cromwell
Illustrated by Dana Regan
Cover illustration by Ron Zalme

Troll

A Creative Media Applications Production

Art Direction by Fabia Wargin Design

Printed in the United States of America. ISBN 0-8167-4320-7

10 9 8 7 6 5 4 3 2 1

What Is the Internet?

The Internet connects many, many computers all around the world. But you can't see the Internet. It's invisible!

Sometimes the Internet is just called the Net. On the Net, a computer can send words, numbers, and pictures to other computers.

Getting onto the Internet

How do you get onto the Internet? You use a computer. Getting onto the Internet is called *going on-line*. You are on-line when your computer connects with another computer already on the Internet.

You also need three other things to hook up to the Net. First, you need a *modem* connected to your computer. Second, you need *software*. Third, you need an *on-line service*.

A modem is a special kind of telephone that lets one computer talk to another computer. Software tells your computer what to do to carry out your commands.

An on-line service is like a post office where you send and receive Internet messages and information. With these three things, you're ready to connect to the Internet.

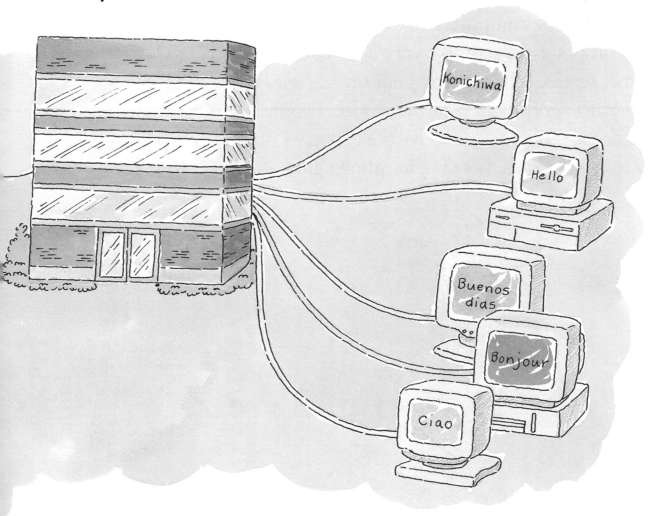

How Things Move on the Internet

When your computer is connected to the Internet, it is connected to thousands of computers all over the world. Messages from your computer are sent to a very large computer at your Internet service. From there, your service sends the messages on to other services all over the world. People who are hooked up to those services can receive the messages no matter where they live, as long as there is a telephone line.

Because computers speak a special language, they can all talk to each other, even though they may be in different parts of the world.

Stay Safe on the Internet

You need to stay safe on the Internet. These three rules will help you stay safe.

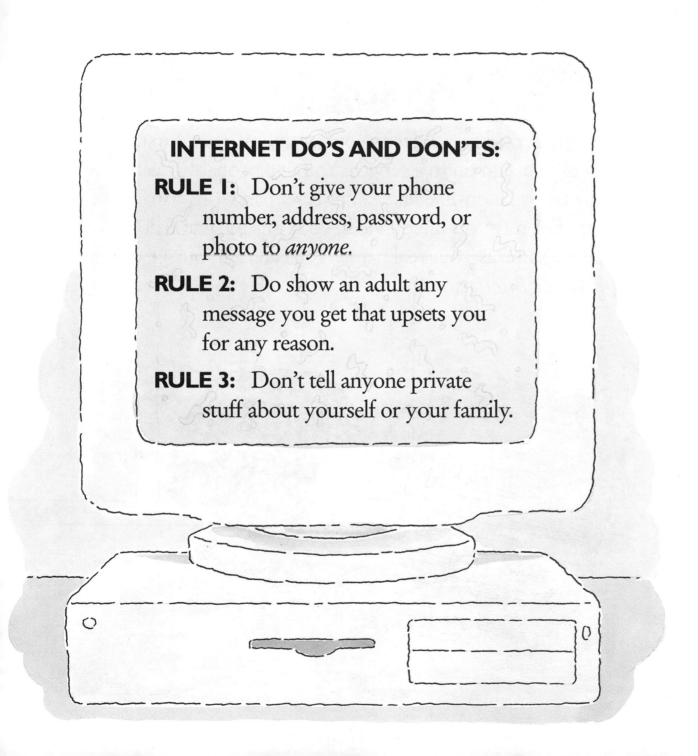

INTERNET DO'S AND DON'TS:

RULE 1: Don't give your phone number, address, password, or photo to *anyone*.

RULE 2: Do show an adult any message you get that upsets you for any reason.

RULE 3: Don't tell anyone private stuff about yourself or your family.

Signing On

You must use an on-line service to contact the Internet. First, ask an adult to help you sign on to a service. You will probably need to set up your own special on-line name and secret password before you can sign on. For most on-line services, your on-line name doesn't have to be the same as your real name. You can call yourself anything, like *Superkid* or *Braniac*.

Each time you sign on to your service, you will have to enter your on-line name and your secret password. Some on-line services go straight to the Internet. With other services, you will have to select the Internet connection after you sign on. Either way, once you sign on and connect to the Internet, you're ready to surf!

Sending E-mail

E-mail is electronic mail, or mail sent on the Internet. You use E-mail to send a note or a letter to someone on the Internet. E-mail can reach a computer anywhere in the world—from your friend's house down the block to the home of a relative who lives in another country!

You need the other person's E-mail address to send E-mail. The E-mail address starts with that person's on-line name. After the on-line name comes the symbol @. Next comes the place where the person has an electronic mailbox. Then, after you send your E-mail, it goes to the person's electronic mailbox. From there, your E-mail goes to the person's computer.

Chat Rooms

You can find new friends on the Internet! A *chat room* is a place to meet people. But a chat room isn't a real room. It's a connection between people who have computers.

There are chat rooms just for kids. In a chat room, your computer is connected, or hooked up, to the computers of other kids in the same room. You use your keyboard to talk instead of using your voice. You type words on your keyboard to talk to other kids in the chat room.

Surfing the Net

Surfing in the ocean means riding the waves on a surfboard. *Surfing the Net* means going from one place to another on the Internet. Your computer is like a surfboard when you surf the Net.

LEARN PLAY NATURE NEWS TRAVEL INFORMATION GAMES

The Internet has lots of words, numbers, pictures, and photos on it. In fact, it has millions of pieces of information. Much of this information is joined in a big collection called the *World Wide Web*.

The World Wide Web

The World Wide Web is made up of a lot of special locations on the Internet that are all connected together. Each Web location is called a *Web site.* Many government agencies, companies, and universities have interesting Web sites you can visit.

Each Web site has one or more *pages.* A page is a screen filled with information about the Web site.

Many Web sites are connected to other Web pages. We say these pages are *linked.* You click on buttons or *icons* on Web pages to go to other linked pages. An icon is a small picture that stands for a program or other computer function.

Visiting a Web Site

Here is how you can visit a Web site. Every Web site has an address, which is called the *URL.* You type the URL into the computer to get to the Web site.

Let's say you want to visit Troll's Web site for the first time. First, you type **http://www.troll.com** into the computer. (You may want to ask an adult to help you type it the first time.) The URL must be typed *exactly* the right way for you to reach the Web site.

When you are done visiting Troll's Web site, just type another URL to go to a new Web site. Now you're surfing the Net!

What Is a Home Page?

When you visit a Web site, the first thing you see is the *home page*. This is the home base for the site. Most home pages have buttons or icons you click on to go to other linked pages.

Some home pages have games, animation, music, and movies connected to icons or buttons. Sometimes you can go to another Web site by clicking on a home page button. When you visit a home page, read the instructions and explore.

Fun Web Sites to Visit

A PLACE TO GO

The White House
URL: **http://www.whitehouse.gov**

See the White House, where the President and his family live. This Web site has a section just for kids. Click on the **White House for Kids** button to see what's there. Then click on buttons for **White House Kids** and **White House Pets**.

THINGS TO DO

The Global Show-n-Tell Museum
URL:
http://www.telenaut.com/gst/

Kids from around the world share their artwork on-line. Follow the instructions on the screen to learn how to add your own artwork to this Web site.

MORE THINGS TO DO

Nikolai's Web Site

URL: **http://www.nikolai.com/nnn.htm**

Here's a place to have fun and learn! You will find stories, crafts, and activities at this Web site. Check out the **ABCD's of Learning**, too.

TO FIND MORE SITES

URL: **http://www.cochran.com/theosite/KSites.html**

This is a listing of many, many Web sites for kids. Each site is rated on a scale of 1 to 5. A 5 rating means that site is really cool!

Glossary

@ This symbol is used in E-mail addresses. It means *at*.

chat room Electronic "room" where people use computers to talk to each other.

downloading Copying a file from another computer to your computer.

E-mail Electronic mail, or notes that are sent from one computer to another using a modem.

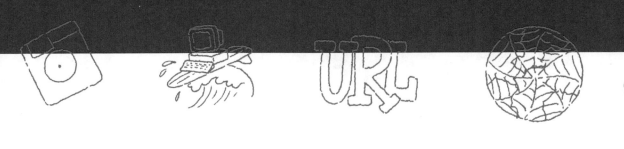

home page The first thing you see when you open a Web site. A home page often tells what you can find at the site.

Internet A group of many, many computers all over the world that are all connected to each other.

link A connection between two Web pages. You can go from one Web page to another by clicking on a link.

modem Your computer's telephone. Your computer uses a modem to connect to other computers.

Net Another word for the Internet.

network A group of computers that are connected to each other. The Internet is the largest network in the world.

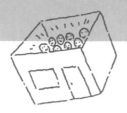

on-line   Where you are when your computer is connected to the Internet.

on-line service   A group of computers that you can connect to by using your modem. You use an on-line service to get onto the Internet.

software   The programs that tell your computer how to carry out the commands you give it. The programs may be for word processing, art, music, games, education, or many other things.

surfing the Net   Using the Internet to explore more than one Web site or topic.

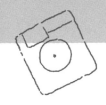

uploading   Copying a file from your computer to another computer.

user ID   The name you are known by when you are on-line.

URL   The address for a Web page. URL stands for Uniform Resource Locator.

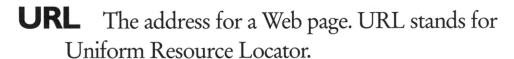

Web page   A single screen in the World Wide Web.

World Wide Web   A huge collection of electronic pages containing information about many different subjects. These pages are stored in computers around the world.

Have fun on the Net!